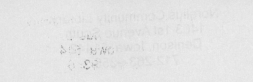

Bugs in my Hair!

David Shannon

The Blue Sky Press • An Imprint of Scholastic Inc. • New York

To moms everywhere
and their battle-tested anti-lice weapons

THE BLUE SKY PRESS

Copyright © 2013 by David Shannon

SCHOLASTIC, THE BLUE SKY PRESS, and associated logos are
trademarks and/or registered trademarks of Scholastic Inc.

Library of Congress catalog card number: 2012042220

ISBN 978-0-545-14313-4

10 9 8 7 6 5 4 3   14 15 16 17

Printed in China   38
First printing, September 2013

One day, my mom made a terrible, awful discovery...

HEaD LiCE!

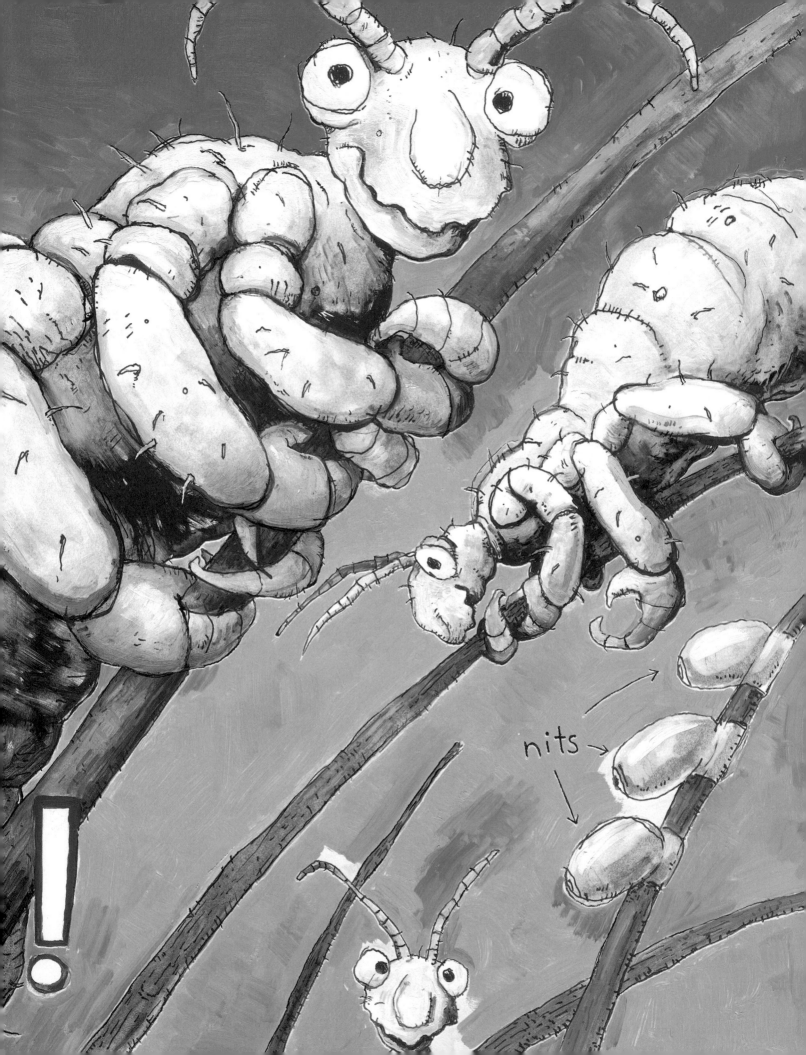

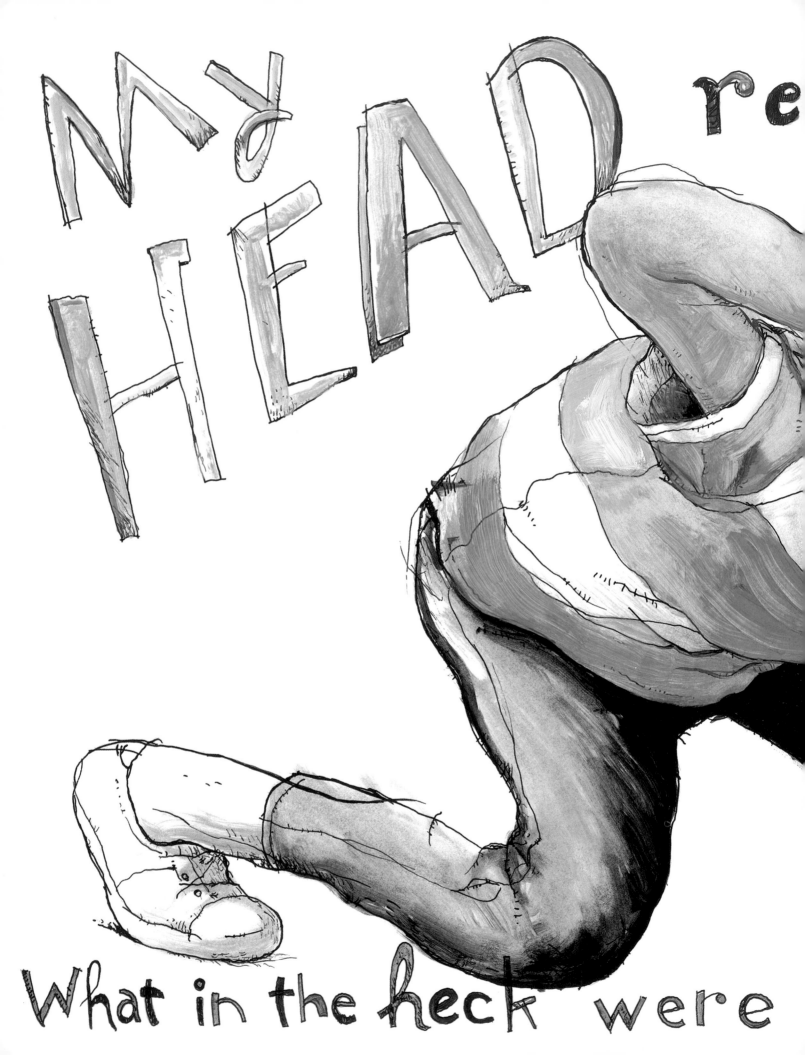

It was hard for some to admit they had lice (even to themselves).

"That's just dandruff."

"I think it's sand from the beach."

"It's probably ash from that volcano in Pogo Pogo."

Other people thought they had lice even when they didn't. Just talking about bugs made my mom itchy. Her problem wasn't <u>on</u> her head, it was <u>in</u> her head!

lots of cures.

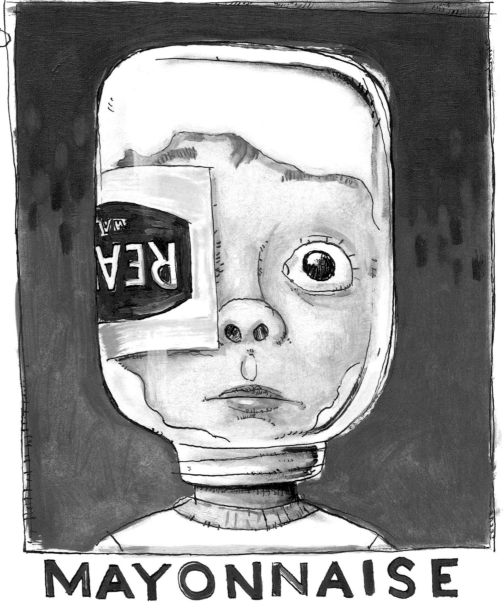

MAYONNAISE

nded AWFUL!

Lice are really hard to get rid of.

Mom read lots of books and magazines and she armed herself with battle-tested anti-lice weapons.

Finally, everything was
laundered, treated, sprayed,
combed, picked,* and cleaned.
We went to a professional
lice treatment place and
I was pronounced bug-free!

* Guess where we get the term "nitpicking."

For the first time in forever
I got a good night's sleep.

And then...

So we went through the whole thing again and now, at last, those awful, disgusting lice are completely gone. And this time...

I'm not taking any chances!